Katie Woo's

Neighborhood

Katie's Vet Loves Pets

by Fran Manushkin

illustrated by Laura Zarrin

PICTURE WINDOW BOOKS
a capstone imprint

Katie Woo's Neighborhood is published by Picture Window Books,
a Capstone imprint
1710 Roe Crest Drive
North Mankato, Minnesota 56003
www.capstonepub.com

Text © 2020 Fran Manushkin
Illustrations © 2020 Picture Window Books

Cataloging-in-Publication data is available on the
Library of Congress website.
ISBN: 978-1-5158-4816-5 (library binding)
ISBN: 978-1-5158-5876-8 (paperback)
ISBN: 978-1-5158-4820-2 (eBook PDF)

Summary: When Katie finds a lost, sick kitten, she and her father take it to the local vet.

Graphic Designer: Bobbie Nuytten

Printed and bound in the USA.
PA100

Table of Contents

Chapter 1
A Lost Kitten

"Meow! Meow! Meow!"

A kitten was crying.

Katie saw her hiding under

a bush.

The kitten was alone.

"You need a home," said
Katie. "When Dad comes
back from work, I'll ask him
what to do."

Katie's friends skated by.
She told them, "This cat
needs a home."

"I already have two cats," said JoJo.

"I have a dog," said Pedro.

"My dad is allergic to cats."

"I want a big fluffy

poodle," said Haley. "But

my mom says six kids are

enough for one small house."

When Katie's dad came
home from work, he said,
"This kitten is very sick.
She may die. We can't take
home a sick kitten."

Katie asked her dad,

"Can we take her to the vet?

Dr. Wong saved Pedro's dog

when he was sick."

"All right," said Katie's

dad. "Let's try."

Chapter 2

At the Vet

Dr. Wong's waiting room

was filled with pets.

Miss Winkle was holding

her dog, Twinkle. "He comes

for his shots every year."

Katie's friend Barry was
with his iguana.

"Zorba is sick," Barry
said. "He hasn't been eating
his broccoli. Zorba loves
broccoli!"

Roddy was with his

parrot, Rocky.

"I'm worried," said

Roddy. "Rocky stopped

talking. He always has

something to say!"

Katie and her dad went in to see Dr. Wong. He picked up the kitten.

He looked in her ears and her eyes and her mouth.

"You came just in time," said Dr. Wong. "This kitten has a bad infection. I'll give her medicine to help her feel better."

Dr. Wong told Katie,

"You must give your kitten

medicine every day."

Katie looked at her dad.

"*Is* she my kitten?"

"Yes!" Her dad smiled.

"Yay!" Katie hugged

her dad.

Dr. Wong told her, "Your

kitten should be feeling

peachy in a week or two."

"*Peachy!*" said Katie.

"That's a perfect name!"

"A very cool name,"
agreed her dad. "She's the
same color as a peach."

Chapter 3
Everything's Peachy

Dr. Wong said, "Some pets do not get well. They are too sick or old. That makes me sad. But most of the time, my job makes me happy."

Katie told him, "I hope
you can help my friends'
dog and parrot and iguana."

"I'll try," said Dr. Wong.

"I love all the animals."

Katie told her friends,

"Meet my new kitten, Peachy."

"Peachy! Peachy! *PEACHY!*"

said Roddy's parrot.

"You are talking!" yelled

Roddy. "You are *not* sick!"

Katie took good care
of Peachy. Every day she
gave Peachy medicine and
food and lots of love.

Peachy got
better and
better. So did
Barry's iguana.

Roddy's parrot
could not stop talking!

Katie could not stop
talking too. She told her
friends, "Dr. Wong will
always help us keep our
pets well."

And he did!

Glossary

allergic (uh-LUR-jik)—if you are allergic to something, it causes you to sneeze, get a rash, or have another unpleasant reaction

iguana (i-GWAN-uh)—a large tropical lizard that has a ridge down its back and can grow to more than five feet in length

infection (in-FEK-shuhn)—an illness caused by germs or viruses

medicine (MED-uh-suhn)—a drug or other substance used in treating illness

peachy (PEECH-y)—very good

Katie's Questions

1. What traits make a good veterinarian? Would you like to be a vet? Why or why not?

2. Katie and her friends were careful not to touch the kitten at the start of the book. Why do you think that is?

3. The vet says that the kitten will be "peachy" after taking her medicine for a while. *Peachy* is a way to say something is very good. Write a sentence using the word *peachy* this way.

4. Make a list of characters and their pets that are mentioned in the story. Which pet would you most like to have? Why?

5. Compare vets and doctors. How are they the same? How are they different?

Katie Interviews a Vet

Katie: Hi, Dr. Wong! Thanks for talking to me about your job. It seems like a great job. What do you like best about it?
Dr. Wong: Ever since I was a little boy, I have loved animals. With my job, I get to meet lots of different animals. Every single one is special.

Katie: I love animals too! Maybe I should be a vet. Would I have to work really hard?
Dr. Wong: I do tend to work long hours, and sometimes I have to work on weekends. Animals don't know that they can only get hurt or sick during my office hours. But I love my job, so I don't mind the hard work.

Katie: That's good. If I decided to go through with this vet thing, would I have to go to school a long time?
Dr. Wong: Well, yes, it takes about eight years. First you must go to college, and then you have to go to veterinary college. It is hard to get into vet school, though. You need to get good grades in college and take lots of science classes.

Katie: Wow! Eight years of college is a long time.

Dr. Wong: It is, but I had a lot of things to learn. I needed to learn how to care for animals of all types and sizes. In one day, I might need to operate on a dog, figure out why a lizard isn't eating, and sew up a horse's cut leg. I need to know how to treat all those different animals.

Katie: Wait! Do people bring their horses to the vet clinic?!

Dr. Wong: No, for large animals like horses or cows, I take trips to the owners' farms. Can you imagine a cow on my exam table?

Katie: Actually, I can, and it is very funny! Thanks again for meeting with me, Dr. Wong. And thanks for taking care of Peachy.

About the Author

Fran Manushkin is the author of Katie Woo, the highly acclaimed fan-favorite early-reader series, as well as the popular Pedro series. Her other books include *Happy in Our Skin, Baby, Come Out!* and the best-selling board books *Big Girl Panties* and *Big Boy Underpants.* There is a real Katie Woo: Fran's great-niece, who doesn't get into trouble like the Katie in the books. Fran lives in New York City, three blocks from Central Park, where she can often be found bird-watching and daydreaming. She writes at her dining room table, without the help of her two naughty cats, Chaim and Goldy.

About the Illustrator

Laura spent her early childhood in the St. Louis, Missouri, area. There she explored creeks, woods, and attic closets, climbed trees, and dug for artifacts in the backyard, all in preparation for her future career as an archeologist. She never became one, however, because she realized she's much happier drawing in the comfort of her own home while watching TV. When she was twelve, her family moved to the Silicon Valley in California, where she still resides with her very logical husband and teen sons, and their illogical dog, Cody.